HERE COMES THE STRIKEOUT

Library of Congress Catalog Number: 65-10728
ISBN 0-06-444011-7
First Harper Trophy edition, 1978.

HERE COMES THE STRIKEOUT

by LEONARD KESSLER

A Sports I CAN READ Book

A Harper Trophy Book

HARPER & ROW, PUBLISHERS

TO MY FAVORITE BASEBALL PEOPLE
OF YESTERDAY AND TODAY:

Arky Vaughan   *Mickey Mantle*
Pie Traynor   *Paul Kessler*
Paul Waner   *Bobby Halberstam*
Honus Wagner   *David Ansell*
Casey Stengel   *Jed Fishman*
Willie Mays   *Sue Carr*

Sluggers 0

Bobcats 0

HERE COMES THE STRIKEOUT

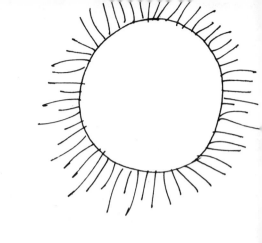

In the spring

the birds sing.

The grass is green,

and boys run and play.

Some boys run
this way.
Some boys run
that way.

And some boys run

to play

B A S E B A L L .

Bobby plays baseball too.

He can run the bases fast.

He can slide.

He can catch the ball.

Sometimes.

But he cannot

hit the ball.

He has *never*

hit the ball.

"Twenty times at bat
and twenty strikeouts,"
said Bobby.
"I am in a bad slump."

14

"Try my good-luck hat

the next time

you come to bat,"

said Willie.

"Thank you," said Bobby.

"I hope it will help me

get a hit."

"Boo, Bobby,"

yelled the other team.

"Easy out.

Easy out.

Here comes the strikeout."

"He can't hit."

"Give him the fast ball."

Bobby stood at home plate

and waited.

The first pitch

was a fast ball.

"Strike one."

The next pitch

was very slow.

Bobby swung hard,

but he missed.

"Strike two."

"Boo! Strike him out!"

"I will hit it this time,"

said Bobby.

He stepped out

of the batter's box.

He took off the lucky hat.

He put it back on.

He stepped back

into the batter's box.

He waited for the pitch.

19

It was a fast ball

right over the plate.

Bobby swung.

"STRIKE THREE!

You are OUT!"

The game was over.

Bobby's team had

lost the game.

"I did it again,"

said Bobby.

"Twenty-one times at bat.

Twenty-one strikeouts.

Take back your lucky hat, Willie.

It was not lucky for me."

It was not a good day

for Bobby.

He had missed

two fly balls.

One dropped out

of his glove.

And one went

over his head.

He had struck out three times.

And his team

had lost the game.

He walked home alone.

"How was the game?"

asked his mother.

"Oh, it was fine,"

said Bobby.

"Time for a nice

hot bath," said his mother.

Bobby went up

to take his bath.

He sat in the tub.

He was not happy.

"Twenty-one times at bat.

Twenty-one strikeouts,"

he said.

And then he began to cry.

"Are you all right in there?"

called his mother.

"I am fine," cried Bobby.

"Then why are you crying?"

asked his mother.

"I'm not crying,"

said Bobby.

"What is the matter, then?"

asked his mother.

"Oh, every time I play baseball,

all I do is strike out.

No one wants me

on the team.

They even choose

the little kids

before they choose me.

They always choose me last."

He sobbed again.

"I wish I were a good hitter."

27

"You can be

a good hitter too,"

said his mother.

"You are a good swimmer.

You are a good runner.

You must work until

you are a good hitter."

"Maybe Willie will help me.

He is a good hitter.

I will ask him," said Bobby.

"Good," said his mother.

"And one more thing.

Did you wash

your face and your ears?"

The next day

Bobby went to see Willie.

"Sure I will help you

with your hitting,"

said Willie.

"But you must work hard

every day.

Lucky hats won't do it.

Lucky bats won't do it.

Only hard work will do it."

"I will work hard,"

said Bobby.

"I want to be a good hitter."

"First we must choose

a bat for you.

We will choose one that is

not too heavy, not too light,

not too long, but just right.

31

"First you hold the bat

this way,

keep your feet

this way,

and you swing the bat

this way, see.

Now you try it."

Bobby did it.

And he did it again

and again

and again.

"One more time,"

said Willie.

"Keep your eyes

on the ball.

Just try to meet

the ball with the bat.

Don't swing too hard.

Just meet it."

Willie pitched the ball.

Bobby swung the bat

very hard.

He swung so hard

that he fell down.

"Strike one,"

said Willie.

"Let's try it again.

But swing easy."

Willie pitched the ball again.

Bobby swung.

And this time

37

he hit the ball.

He did not hit it very far,

but he hit the ball.

"Good boy," said Willie.

"You hit it. You did it."

"I HIT THE BALL.

I HIT THE BALL,"

said Bobby.

"I HIT IT. I HIT IT.

I CAN DO IT.

I CAN GET A HIT!"

He jumped up and down.

"Let's try it again,"
said Willie.

And that is what they did
all that day,

and the next day,

and the next.

Some days Bobby
worked with Willie.
Some days he
worked alone.

41

Some days he did

a little better.

Some days he did not

do so well.

There were good days.

There were bad days.

But he kept working

and trying.

"I hope I get a hit
in a game," said Bobby.

"You can hit the ball,"
said Willie.

"You will get a hit
in a game."

The next day

was a big game.

Bobby's team was the Bobcats.

The other team was the Sluggers.

The first time Bobby came to bat,

he did what Willie had told him.

He held the bat this way.

He kept his feet this way.

He was ready.

The first pitch was a strike.

On the next pitch Bobby swung.

And he hit the ball.

It was a little pop fly

to the shortstop.

Bobby was out.

"But I hit it,"

said Bobby.

"I will do better next time."

In the last

of the fourth inning

the score was

    Sluggers: Three runs

    Bobcats: Three runs

Then Willie came up to bat.

He hit a long drive

to center field.

"Home run, home run!"

yelled his team.

But a little dog

ran off with the ball.

They had to stop

the game and chase the dog

to get the baseball back.

Then both teams had to rest

from all that running.

It was a long inning.

In the last inning

the score was still

Sluggers: Three runs

Bobcats: Three runs

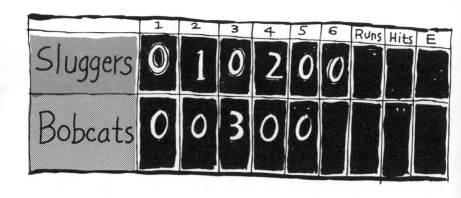

	1	2	3	4	5	6	Runs	Hits	E
Sluggers	0	1	0	2	0	0			
Bobcats	0	0	3	0	0				

It was the last time

at bat for the Bobcats.

There were two outs.

There was a man on third base.

And who was up at bat?

It was Bobby.

"Look who is up,"

yelled the Sluggers.

"HERE COMES THE STRIKEOUT!"

"Move in close. He can't hit it."

"Strike him out."

Bobby held the bat.

"I can do it,"

he said softly.

He swung

and

missed.

"Strike one."

"Move in closer,"

shouted the shortstop.

"He was lucky the last time up."

"He can't hit it again."

Bobby swung.

"Strike two."

"One more strike

and he is out."

The shortstop laughed.

Willie walked up to the plate.

"Get a hit, Bobby.

Just meet the ball,"

said Willie.

"You can do it!"

The pitcher looked over

at the runner on third base.

He looked at Bobby.

And now he was ready.

The pitch came in fast.

Bobby swung his bat.

Crack.

Pow.

Up—up.

Up went the ball

over the head

of the shortstop

and dropped on the grass.

It was a base hit.

"Run, Bobby. Run to first base,"

yelled Willie.

Bobby just stood there.

"Run! Run! Run!"

the Bobcats screamed.

Bobby started to run.

He ran fast.

"Safe!"

The runner on third base

had crossed home plate

with the winning run.

The game was over.

The Bobcats had won.

"Good hit, Bobby,"

said Willie.

"Good hit,"

said the other boys.

"Twenty-three times at bat.

Twenty-one strikeouts,

one pop fly,

and ONE HIT."

Bobby smiled at Willie.

When he came home

his mother asked,

"How was the game?"

Bobby smiled.

"I got a hit.

We won the game."

"Wonderful!" said his mother.

Now when Bobby plays baseball,

sometimes he strikes out.

But most times he hits the ball.

"How do you do it?" asked Larry.

"A lucky bat?" said Paul.

"No," said Bobby.

"Lucky bats won't do it.

Lucky hats won't do it.

Only hard work will do it."

He looked at Willie,

and they laughed.